# AN AETHERIAL WAR SHORT STORY COLLECTION VOLUME 2

# An Aetherial War Short Story Collection Volume 2

**NATHAN DOVERSPIKE**

Nathan Earl Doverspike

# CONTENTS


*Dedication*     vii

1   The Toughest Goodbye     1

2   Zeroes and Ones     4

3   Damaged Goods     8

4   Mutual Goals     12

5   Purpose     16

6   The Tinkerer     21

7   The Will To Survive     25

*About The Author*     29

This story wouldn't be possible without the encouragement and support from my parents, loving wife, and amazing friends. To Jaina, never stop believing in your dreams and striving to be great.

We do what we must. Because we must.

# | 1 |

# The Toughest Goodbye



*Nineteen years before the events of The Edge of Madness*

*Don't show him you care. Don't show him how hurt you are by this reckless choice. You can do it. Hold it together, girl. He will come around on it. He must.*

Nayomi inhaled mightily and exhaled her frustration at the man standing in front of her with the front door open. Her white knuckles shook with rage, but she kept her face as stoic as possible. Only the slight narrowing of her eyes gave an obvious sign that she couldn't believe the nonsense coming from his mouth.

The young man with shoulder-length chestnut hair continued to foolishly explain his reasoning. "Look, I know this isn't easy to hear. I love you with every fiber of my being, Nayomi. This isn't easy for me either-"

*Nope, that's it. Now you've done it.*

She couldn't hold her emotions back any longer. "This isn't easy for you?! That's all you can come up with? You're a real bastard, Kai Stormbringer. Times get tough and instead of staying and fighting, you take the coward's way out and run. Where are you going to go? Are you going to change your name? Change your whole identity?"

He stood there, speechless. She could see the hurt in his beautiful blue and gold eyes. A gentle breeze intruded on the argument and blew the bottom of his dumb coat. She hated that coat, so damn much. It looked so ridiculous on him. And yet, she wanted nothing more than to keep it as a memento, if this was their final conversation.

"You know what happened the last time I stood and fought. I nearly died, along with Master Dracken and my own baby brother! I *won't* let that happen to you. If they come for me, and I know they will eventually, I couldn't bear knowing I put you in danger. Not now; not ever."

"You really think they'll come now? It's been over six standard months. If they haven't found you by now, what in the six hells makes you think they have found you?"

He squirmed awkwardly. There was something he wasn't telling her. She couldn't quite put her finger on it, but somehow, he must know they were closing in. And quickly.

She could see the mountains over his shorter stature. The puffy clouds and light brown sky looked painted above them as the bright blue sun began to set. It should have been a moment to enjoy the picturesque landscape; one she would have wanted to enjoy with her husband. Not today.

*How did it come to this? Why did it have to come to this?*

A subconscious decision to shoot her right hand out and grab his wrist as he began to turn away surprised them both. He looked at her hand, then into her eyes. Like his, they swirled like a galaxy inside the lavender-colored irises. A flood of emotions streamed down her beautiful, dark complexion.

"I'm pregnant. I wanted to wait to tell you. Please don't leave. You're my husband, my partner, my best friend. I don't think I can raise this child without you."

A tear rolled down his flushed cheek. He wiped it away quickly with a flash of his hand. Surprisingly, he held her hand in both of his. They still held their eternal warming comfort. "Goodbye, Nayomi. I hope that one day you'll find it in your heart to forgive me and understand this is something I must do. After all, we do what we must, because we must. Right?"

*That's what they always said. And then they abandoned us. Just like you're going to abandon me. Abandon the both of us.*

Kai leaned forward and gently kissed her soft cheek. Nayomi didn't respond. She didn't know how. After one last look into his eyes, he turned and slowly left. As she watched him walk outside, she wondered if she would ever see him again. Or if this was the last goodbye.

Something wasn't right. She didn't need her uncanny ability to sense true feelings through the Aether to notice so many little yet obvious signs. The young Aetherial didn't have his normal confident posture. His shoulders slumped and his head hung low as he walked away. His feet almost dragged on the ground, as if he had to fight against his own will to keep moving forward and not turn around.

He was stubborn. Too stubborn. She knew she couldn't stop him if he made up his mind to leave, so she decided to do the next best thing: give him a reason to stay alive until he changed his mind.

Her voice cracked as she called out to him one last time. "Kai. If they do find you, give them hell. Never forget me. Don't you dare forget us. If you do, I swear by the old gods I will haunt you until the day you join me among the stars. And if today is the day, then make it count."

If it was the last time she saw him, she was sure it would be her toughest goodbye.

# | 2 |

# Zeroes and Ones

*Eleven years before the events of The Edge of Madness*

"It isn't doing anything, Anders. Are you *sure* it is going to work? If not, I need to take her now so I can give her a proper burial." Joren insisted impatiently. The hour was late, and both men were tired, both for entirely different reasons.

Anders couldn't blame him. The lifeless body of Joren's barely teenage daughter lies on the padded and reclined table before them. He couldn't imagine the pain the man was suffering at this difficult time, but he had a rough idea. His parents were taken too soon, slain in cold blood by Crimson Skull thugs looking to make a quick cred off unsuspecting victims. His father had fought back, and paid the ultimate price. His mother's life was taken when she threatened to turn them in to the Galactic Imperium authorities.

That left Anders with very little choice but to take a chance and join the Galactic Imperium. Though he wasn't the most physically gifted in his class, he was good with numbers and his fingers. They danced gracefully across the Holovid keyboard projected beneath the screen illuminated in front of his chubby face. His breath labored from intense concentration mixed with moderate obesity.

"It will work. I ran the numbers hundreds of times already. I know it will work. There must be something I'm missing. Let me run it through one more time."

Joren sighed audibly and leaned his back against a nearby wall, arms crossed and a blank stare brimming with despair aimed at the cold, metal floor. This man was the closest person to a friend that Anders had, and he refused to let him down. Now here. Not now.

On one screen, he dug deep into the program files, looking for any indication of what might be causing the transfer to fail, while on the second screen he ran a few basic scripts to find any open conversations on the Grid that may help in his code troubleshooting. The wires attached to Ava's brain ran into his computer and should be copying her consciousness. It kept failing, which meant something just wasn't right. If even one line of code was incomplete or incorrect, it would certainly prevent it from executing successfully.

As they normally did, Anders eyes bounced wildly across the screens. Back and forth they read expertly crafted code, frantically looking for an error; any error. Though the current situation was dire, his pace was always the same. Nonstop.

"Snowman, I appreciate the effort, but I think we're done here. She deserves a proper burial and I need...I need some time alone." Joren's somber voice interrupted the methodical tapping of stubby fingers on the projected keyboard.

Anders Fleury, whose self-given moniker was Snowman, pushed his oversized glasses back to their proper spot on the bridge of his nose without missing a beat. "Joren, you have to trust me. I know I can do this. I know it will work."

*You have to trust me, Joren. I know this might seem like a far-fetched idea to you, but all my calculations confirmed it should work. I just have to find the error that's holding it up.*

*THERE!*

Just as he finished speaking, he spotted it. Buried deep in the code's foundation was an incorrectly pointed directory. In theory, he should be able to rewrite it to point to a valid databank to complete the upload. With code, theory wasn't always reality, as he all too often found out the hard way.

*Just a few adjustments. Let's redirect that pointer here, and ensure the connection is secured. We don't want anyone to compromise this Grid node and be able to copy the code during transfer or see what we are trying to accomplish. The G.I. has spiders crawling all over the Grid, looking for anything they can report back to Intelligence. Best not to make it too easy for them today.*

A pleasant ding from the Holovid indicated the transfer was successful. Moments passed. Nothing happened. The silence between the two men dragged on as they waited, until Anders couldn't take it any longer.

"It should work! I fixed the error, and the code executed successfully. What the hell else is wrong with this thing?!"

Just then, a voice squeaked out from the Holovid. It wasn't just any voice; it was child-like, almost whimsical in nature, eternally naive to the world around them.

"Hello? Is anyone there? Daddy? Daddy is that you?"

Both men's jaws hit the floor, hard. Neither could believe what they were hearing. They exchanged an incredulous look. As the realization set in, Anders smiled warmly at the broken man at the other end of the room who now stood upright in shock. Usually quite stoic in nature, Anders never thought he would see so much emotion from Joren in his lifetime.

Trying to sound normal, Joren answered, "Give me just one minute, Ava, sweetie. Daddy has a lot to explain."

"Okay, but don't be too long. I think it's past my bedtime."

Joren placed a hand on the shoulder of the master coder, his grip firm with the slightest shake. "I'm going to need some time. Thank you, Snowman. You were right, you did it." Joren met Anders' eyes. The pain mixed with pure bliss created a pressed smile that made Anders shiver from the oddity.

Most would have marveled at the success of his programming expertise. He brought someone back literally from the other side, despite the myriad of claims that he was crazy and it couldn't be done. Few knew about the program, fewer still knew what he was trying to accomplish with it.

Now, he knew they were wrong because tonight, he proved it. Maybe not to them, but to himself. Tonight, that's all that mattered; he performed a quantum physics equivalent of a miracle. Anders metaphorically patted himself on the back as he swiveled off his chair and exited the room.

To the one who preferred the moniker Snowman over his birth name, though, it was still all zeroes and ones.

| **3** |

# Damaged Goods

*Eight years before the events of The Edge of Madness*

"Why the fuck did you pick *this* one up?" growled the Wulvern pirate. His teeth barred at his shorter, and fatter, companion who didn't shy away from the confrontation. Both wore shiny metal piece-meal armor, and hardly any of it matched in color or texture. Some pieces were smooth grey pauldrons, while others were onyx-colored boots and gauntlets. Though their weapons were more technologically advanced, their outfits looked ridiculous to Grimhorn.

"It was the only one we could catch; stupid beast stood right in the damn way, in fact. Look at it, basically harmless in that cage. No wonder its horn is all smashed up like that. Dumb thing probably ran head-first into a boulder."

The pair howled in laughter at the insult; the fatter one bending over as he grasped his overflowing belly.

Rhonar had little need for armor. They were strong warriors, born with armor-like hide on their backs that protected them against most conventional weapons. Grimhorn was no beast. Nor was he, as this puny Wulvern called him, dumb.

Grimhorn's nostrils flared out slightly as he let loose an annoyed snort. It caught their attention, and their furry faces contorted into

8

what Grimhorn assumed was disgust for his kind. They approached the barred metal cage which held the captive Rhonar.

"You got something to say, beast? How quickly I forget, Rhonar are too stupid to communicate with words." He said with a growling hiss.

The fat one chimed in as well. "I heard they are too stupid to mate. That's why their numbers are nearing extinction. Looks like, despite this one being damaged goods, it should still fetch us a fair bounty once we bring him to the Crimson Skulls. They love big, dumb animals for their underground fighting pits."

Grimhorn snarled and glared at them from where he sat against the cold, metal wall. An overwhelming feeling of rage slowly built inside the mammoth being. It churned and boiled within, yet Grimhorn stayed silent. Waiting.

"What, you don't like being trapped in this cage? Too bad, beast. Once we hand you over, then you can unleash your animalistic rage on those poor fuckers."

A smile crept over Grimhorn's mouth. It peeled back his large lips to expose huge, blocky teeth. He grumbled through them, "Grimhorn not stuck in cage. Tiny Wulvern stuck in ship with Grimhorn."

Before either Wulvern could throw another insult, Grimhorn rose, strode to the cage bars, and pried them apart, muscles bulging, until the gap was wide enough to fit his massive frame through.

"Oh shit!" the taller Wulvern exclaimed as he raised his blaster in a futile attempt to defend himself. It belched purple plasma that hurled toward the charging Rhonar. The Rhonar warrior was ready for the attack, and he lowered his shoulder as the blasts dissipated against it harmlessly. The fat Wulvern was significantly wiser as he leaped behind a stack of metal crates for cover. The cover would be no match for Grimhorn, but he did save himself from immediate and certain death.

Before the pirate could pull the trigger again, Grimhorn grabbed onto his neck with a blood-curling roar spun around and smashed the full-sized Wulvern into the ship's floor. The impact left the Wulvern mangled as bones snapped and muscles tore, yet he still breathed raspy gasps for air. Unwilling to allow this inferior warrior a dignified end,

Grimhorn raised the Wulvern's bloodied body so his eyes met his captor's. He snarled with gnashing teeth and a fiery rage burning in his eyes.

"Ppplease...spare me." The captor pleaded. Begging was for the weak, and Grimhorn knew only one way to deal with weak souls.

Grimhorn's eyes narrowed as he spoke slowly. "Grimhorn spares no puny warriors. Grimhorn not broken. Grimhorn still whole." With that, he hurled the limp body towards the ship's wall. If Grimhorn didn't know better, he would have been impressed that the impact pushed the ship in that direction, even if it was only a slight movement. The lifeless body crumpled to the floor; dark blood pooling around the mess of exposed bones through the metal armor.

He turned, slowly turning his attention to the laborious, wheezy mouth-breathing coming from behind the metal crates on the far side of the large room. A stomp of Grimhorn's hoof sent a shockwave of air from the dent in the floor it created. If these captors believed Grimhorn to be a beast, then Grimhorn would act like a beast. A wild, untamed, rage-fueled beast. But Grimhorn refused to be broken.

The Rhonar roared in fury and slammed both fists into the floor, causing the crates to tumble and crash loudly to the floor. Shaking uncontrollably, the fat Wulvern stared with wide eyes in terror at Grimhorn, his friend's body, then back to Grimhorn. His eyes darted to the open door to his right, then again to Grimhorn, knowing that was his only exit.

A large hoof scraped the floor as Grimhorn prepared to charge the weak opponent. He could not allow them to leave and inform the rest of the crew. Without waiting any further, he charged towards the Wulvern, snorting furiously as he ran. The ship trembled under the heavy pounding of his feet.

The fat Wulvern somehow managed to scamper out of the way of the rampaging Rhonar. Clawing at the metal floor, the pirate dove through the doorway and slammed a furry paw on the wall. Sirens blared, almost drowning out a furious roar from Grimhorn. Thick doors with transparent glass in the middle come from both sides of the entryway slammed shut with such force it knocked back the Wulvern onto his rear.

Terrified eyes widened as they watched Grimhorn pace back and forth, his gaze unwavering. He hoped to scare the literal excrement from this being. It prevented him from exacting his revenge on the rest of the poachers. Without a word, Grimhorn sat down and folded his huge hands into his lap.

He knew it was only a matter of time before the ship reached its destination. Until then, he would prepare. He would be ready.

*Grimhorn will wait. Grimhorn will have his revenge.*

# | 4 |

# Mutual Goals

*Six months and five days after the events of Chaos and Consequences*

*SCHUNK!*

Her massive blade bit deep into her opponent's furry brown chest, severing flesh, sinew, and bone. The once-intimidating in appearance Volkoth went limp, and she used her metallic right foot to gain some leverage as she yanked the blade back out with a gross gurgle from the being. It crashed to the sticky mix of cracked concrete and dirt beneath her feet with a loud thud. With four arms and impressive size, they fell like trees in a wicked storm. Her blade dimly reflected some of the blinking neon signs above, creating a strange palette of bright orange and teal with matte crimson.

"We done yet? I think we've done enough damage to their—well, what I think was-their gang." The beautiful voice belonging to a fresh recruit on her watch called from behind. The blonde woman was shorter in stature, but built solid with tanned muscles, and was quick with her rifle. A smirk pulled the right crease between her soft lips back, making her even more stunning in the fading sunlight. Despite her attraction to this beauty, Talia knew she couldn't break her one rule.

*Never get too attached.*

Doing so cost her a leg, and that wouldn't have been the only thing she lost had she refused to allow herself those kinds of relationships. Those only ended in heartbreak for both parties, and she didn't want to go through that again.

"Yeah, I think we can go." She replied as calloused hands wiped gore and brown fur off her one-of-a-kind blade. "You hungry?" As if on cue, Talia's stomach let out a series of gurgles and groans.

The recruit nodded in affirmation as a sudden realization surfaced at the forefront of her mind. It had surprised Talia when this woman showed up to a recruitment party wearing G.I. gear, and even more shocking when she was the only one left standing. Usually, the G.I. are the first to fall, but not this one. This one had something she was fighting for, or someone worth dying for.

As the pair turned to leave the alley, a quick series of chirps rang out from Talia's device strapped to her wrist. The square communication device was bulkier than newer models and had inferior technological features, but it was significantly more durable. In her line of work, that advantage couldn't be overstated.

A few button presses later and a blue outline apparated hovering above the device. The dark setting and glowing eyes immediately gave away the caller, and she fought back a shiver and a lump in her throat.

*Underlord Redbeard.*

"So, you're the one disrupting my supply chain out there," the voice said calmly but icy cold. "Your physique is more, intimidating, than I would have imagined. Wearing the fur of one of my former guards as a cape, now *that's* bold." She thought she saw a tiny smirk from him, but it disappeared just as quickly. The cape draped over her shoulders was from a formidable Volkoth she defeated, though she had no idea it was one of Redbeard's thugs. Had she known, she likely would have avoided that job altogether.

He had a way of knowing almost everything, and slithering into situations where he was the utmost uninvited guest.

*Don't hesitate and don't be too arrogant. Let's just be cool and see what he wants. Maybe it's a courtesy call. Probably not, though.*

"Underlord Redbeard. It's nice to finally speak with you. Glad you like my wardrobe, but we both know that isn't why you called." Now she noticed a smile crease his lips without a doubt; his eyes blazing intensely through the projection.

"How very insightful. No, that isn't why I'm contacting you. I have a particularly long thorn in my side, and who better to remove it than a slightly less irritating pest who is disrupting my entirely legal operations. Before you reject the offer, let me show you the target."

The projection phased into that of a floating male head, likely in his thirties or early forties with hair that changed color about halfway to the roots. The gaunt features and baggy eyes matched that of someone she thought was on the run from the G.I. His eyes, though, were something she had never seen before. It looked like stars sparkled inside each iris, like they held the secrets of the universe within.

Out of the corner of her eye, Talia spotted her recruit's eyes narrow and the color drain from her face. Either she had seen this man before, or at least knew of him. That was enough reason to give this a second thought.

A handful of moments passed before Redbeard continued. "This is Kai Stormbringer. I want him, and anyone with him, delivered to me; in one piece, preferably. So, what's your answer?"

*If she's interested, then so am I. There must be a reason her expression changed so quickly in a moment.*

"What's the bounty?"

"Five."

"Thousand? Not worth my time."

"You didn't let me finish, Talia. Five million."

*Holy shit. Now that's a number I can work with.*

"Deal. Give me some time to get a crew and supplies together."

"You have two weeks. He is already on his way to Valorium. I set up a special welcoming spot for them. I'll send over the coordinates. Good luck, Talia Ironwood. Try not to die too quickly."

The call ended before she could respond. She gulped hard, and shot a curious look with a raised brow at her new companion.

*Damn, what was her name again? I figured this would be our first and only raid. My memory sure isn't what it was a few decades ago. Maybe I can casually find out, so it isn't so jarring.*

"So, recruit, that was some mildly impressive work you pulled off. What did you say your name was again?"

A brow raised on the woman's soft features showed her mild surprise. "Never thought you'd ask. Didn't take you for one to get to know someone, considering the job and all. Name's Em."

Talia offered out a hand, and smiled widely when the gesture was returned with a firm handshake from Em. One of Talia's giant hands nearly enveloped Em's, but the grasp was just as strong from the smaller woman.

Em smiled slightly, her face glowing in the odd lighting from the dilapidated town. "It looks like we have a mutual goal, Talia. Happy to be part of the crew, even if it is just the two of us."

Talia's heart skipped a beat in excitement, though her expression never changed. She nodded in agreement and led the way out towards the nearest pub for a well-deserved drink and grub. "Let me buy you a drink, and you can tell me all about this Stormbringer character."

*Don't get too attached. You never know what danger lurks around the corner, especially in a backwater plant like Brae.*

*We have mutual goals, and let's keep it at that.*

# | 5 |

# Purpose

*Nearly seven months after the events of Chaos and Consequences*

For as long as he could remember, he wondered who he had been before. Clouded memories surface every now and again, but nothing concrete. Nothing that would give him a sign of his true purpose; of why someone brought him back to life. Not once. Not twice. Not a hundred times.

Over, and over, and over again. He was brought back. From where, he had no idea. Despite what he assumed were thousands of ultimate ends, what awaited beyond never presented itself. Perhaps that's exactly what it was: the end. Absolute nothingness. An absolute end. One moment he was drawing his last breath, the next, his first started again.

The thought chilled him slightly. After all, there had to be something after, right? There had to be another existence, or a new beginning for one's soul, their literal essence to materialize into. If not, what's the point of existing in the first place?

Sounds of glass shattering in the distance followed quickly by sudden shouting brought him back from his drifting consciousness. Something wasn't right. He felt it in his core that beat in place of his heart. Emerald pulses quickened from within as the metal rings rapidly rotated around, as if warning him to danger. A tip from an anonymous source spoke of possible Resistance members hiding out in an abandoned warehouse on Brae, where the tall, dark-skinned man found himself standing now.

He had been given strict orders before his group entered the building. "Stay here." The powerful Aetherial male had commanded him. "Don't leave this spot, no matter what, you understand?"

As far as he could remember now, he never spoke a word, though he did nod slightly in acknowledgment. The Aetherial male of slightly shorter stature and pale skin patted him solidly on the shoulder before leading the rest of the group inside the huge warehouse.

*Words need to hold a purpose, otherwise they are needless noises. I may not speak, but when I do, it will be with purpose.*

Since this group of various species and misfits rescued him from his seemingly eternal slumber, he had rarely made any choices. He had gone along with any plans, followed any commands, and done as told. But what if that had led him to his original end? The very first one that he; at least vaguely believes, ended with gunfire and screams. Was it due to action, or inaction?

Despite focusing as best he could, the man could not remember.

He also could not stand if these beings were in danger. They protected him at all costs, sometimes against unimaginable odds, without hesitation.

*Why? Why do they continue to put their lives at risk for my own? Is my single life worth of all theirs combined? Do I hold secrets they know and are unwilling to divulge? If so, what would those secrets reveal regarding who I am, or what I am?*

*I must find out. I must know who I am, and the reasons behind always being brought back from the brink of existence. My lost past may always haunt my memories, but the only chance I have at remembering is keeping these Aetherials and my maker alive.*

*I have made my choice. Harm will not befall you today, Aetherials.*

His body reacted without his mind needing to direct it. A left shoulder slammed open the door, bursting it off its hinges as it clanged onto the floor beside him. His eyes darted back and forth, scanning the scenery for where they may be. Shouting and what sounded like mini explosions shook the ground beneath his bare feet. He took off through the cluttered entrance in the direction from which he hoped they originated.

Weaving back and forth through desolate hallways, the rhythmic patting of his feet propelled him by empty rooms from what looked like centuries of neglect and abandonment covered each one in a blanket of dust and rust. As his arms pumped back and forth and his feet carried him forward toward the increasingly louder commotion, he wondered if he had been a worker in a place like this. Was his prior life, or lives for that matter, filled with satisfaction, or were they ravaged with a monotonous misery?

He knew he would never find the answer. Even if he did, would he want to know? Or would his past shake him to the core within his chest from an existential crisis?

Before his thoughts overwhelmed him, as they often threatened to do since he awoke six months ago, the winding hallways opened suddenly into a massive production room. The floor was covered with conveyor belts and what appeared to be welding stations, while the outside walls were lined with thousands of small glass windows, though a good portion of them were smashed or cracked. With a quick glance around, he could tell it was once an impressive factory that rivaled anything he witnessed on the Core planets in scale.

At the epicenter of the massive facility, a battle of blue and different hues of purple magic wreaked havoc among the machinery. Volleys back and forth of the devastating blasts left smoldering holes wherever they struck, be it glass or metal. Light and dark purple blasts continued to fly, but the azure ones he grew accustomed to seeing from the sometimes-ornery Aetherial master subsided.

Intertwining tentacles of dark purple material blocked shot after shot from the former Galactic Imperium detective Joren Steel's blasters. Despite the huge man's persistent shower of plasma belching from the guns, the tall being seemed to be able to anticipate each one, intercepting them with one of the multiple flailing appendages.

It was then he spotted the Aetherial named Kai Stormbringer motionless on the ground as weird tentacles protruding from behind a tall, hooded being wrapped themselves around his body and retrieved it. Even from this distance away, the man could see a wicked smile creep over the being's gaunt face as he slung the body over his shoulder.

The other shorter Aetherial, Lily as most called her, yelled in anger as she threw her glowing daggers towards the aggressor. It batted them away, sending them clattering to the floor harmlessly. She snarled and cursed at him continuously sending spittle flying with unbridled rage.

An emotion surfaced from the depths of his mind. It was strange, foreign, yet somehow familiar enough to bring him a little warmth of comfort. He closed his eyes. The emotion intensified as he continued focusing on it, allowing it to consume his thoughts, to take control and guide his movements.

The core within him hummed audibly with power as the emerald Aether powering it flowed down his arms that hung by his side. The feeling was nearly overwhelming, overtaking every fiber of his being and guiding his movements in a way he found almost cathartic.

*So, this is what it's like? To feel pure power in its most absolute form is exhilarating.*

The strange being pointed a long finger at the man bathed in green Aether and spoke in an almost too-calm tone amid the chaos. "You're not an Aetherial, at least not one I've felt the presence of through the Aether. You clearly aren't completely organic, though, either. So then, stranger, what the *fuck* are you?" The humanoid being hissed through the dark hood masking his face. The motionless form of Kai Stormbringer hung over the man's long shoulder.

As emerald Aether wrapped itself around him in its warm embrace, pulsating from the Aetherial Core embedded in his chest, the man spoke with purpose. "My name is Malik Maholmes. You will leave this place, interloper. Or I will see that you meet your maker today."

A crooked smile parted the hooded man's lip as he lifted his hood back. Abyssal darkness replaced his pupils as the dark purple Aether illuminated his gaunt and pale facial features. Though he was human in form, the lack of pupils gave him an otherworldly appearance, even to Malik. He narrowed his eyes on the aggressor, ready for a fight.

Tendons popped from clenched fists as the man obliged by cracking his neck from side to side. "As you wish, Malik Maholmes. We will see how long you last."

*I will last as long as needed, stranger. I now know my purpose, and I will not cease until it is accomplished.*

# | 6 |

## The Tinkerer



*Seven months after the events of Chaos and Consequence*

"Wrong. All wrong." The elderly male Praug croaked in frustration at his shaky, webbed hands. As the years passed, the slight tremble in them had grown increasingly worse, making it more and more difficult to do the only thing at which he knew he could do. Fix things.

His workshop was very modest, a handful of tables where he could work on any ad hoc jobs that came his way, provided they weren't requested by the Galactic Imperium. He had a personal grudge against them, and this Praug held on to grudges for far longer than he likely would admit out loud. A waist-high counter near the front allowed him to greet any guests that stumbled across his business. The door in the back was locked with an advanced biometric scanner, requiring both an iris and fingerprint to open. He didn't want anyone just waltzing into his attached apartment, after all.

As he tinkered with the damaged synthetic humanoid separated into numerous pieces on his metal table, he wondered to himself if he would ever be lucky enough to work on something more meaningful. Putting together busted synths kept food in his stomach, sure, but there was more to this life. He knew there was. Years ago, he had a purpose, had peers he could trust, and a meaningful place in the galaxy.

Now? Now, he was stuck on some backwater, hellhole planet called Valorium in the far reaches of the galaxy called the Fringe. Technically, it could be worse. He could be dead, or rotting in Darklight Prison. It wasn't much of a consolation, but it was something. Though he could certainly do with more water around, and less ravaging wind storms that coats everything with coarse dust. He hated dust.

His eyes squinted, his hands trembled slightly as he continued to weld and wire the tiny mechanical circuit boards inside the synth's chest. Despite it losing most of its lubrication fluid from a royal smashing by some local Galactic Imperium miscreants, it still retained that metallic scent. It filled the Praug's slanted nostrils as they flared open and closed quickly. Most Praug were strictly against artificial intelligence, believing that it was an abomination against science.

KarDel wasn't most Praug, though. Most Praug wouldn't leave their greatest creation behind to transplant themselves onto a remote planet hostile in more ways than one.

*They really gave you a good beating, didn't they? Let me guess, you refused to obey their orders because it would have put you in a situation that would have likely resulted in your termination? That's typical of them. Damn brutes. Even out here in the Fringe, their stench fouls the air we breathe.*

*Maybe I was better off on Praug.*

The jarring thought forced him to stop his work. No, he wasn't better off back on Praug. He would have been put to work by those Galactic Imperium oppressors, forced to create weapons of death and destruction. He liked to tinker and discover more efficient ways to make things work. He didn't like to create things that were capable of *killing* another living being. The last project he had a hand in creating on Praug was the final straw. Sure, it was ultimately a success after years of trial and error. But at what cost?

He worked with a brilliant, young Praug woman. Cunning, headstrong, fierce, and a little crazy at times. She loved her work and it showed. They made a great team, and at one point he had hoped they would become more than that. He missed her more than anything.

*Those days are over. Better to leave them behind where they belong than reminisce about better memories.*

With an involuntary grunt, he hobbled towards a nearby wall with countless tools hung on small protruding pegs. His gimp from a prosthetic metal leg was a reminder of his past, and why he would never work for the Galactic Imperium again. He tried to split ways with them peacefully. They instead chose violence, as was their usual preference. He grabbed a smaller wire splicer, a bottle of synth fluid, and made his gimpy way back to the table to continue his work.

As he often was, KarDel was left with only his thoughts, his tools, and his projects to keep him company. It wasn't until a throat cleared loudly behind him that he hobbled until he was facing the entryway. Before him stood someone he never expected to see again.

"Tu'Mar?" He couldn't believe his eyes. They widened at the presence of someone he had missed seeing every day. Praug weren't overly emotional beings, but even he felt a tear well up in his eyes. She had a few more stress wrinkles on her neck, and her clothing resembled a field worker with its earthy colors against her orange skin. But without a doubt, it was still her.

A genuine smile spread across Tu'Mar's lips; that same twinkle in her eyes warmed his old soul. "It's good to see you again, KarDel. Or should I say, Tinkerer?"

He croaked out a raspy laugh. "I haven't heard that name in a long time, friend. It's almost as good to hear it as it is to see you. When I got the news that our old facility was destroyed by that madman Demico, I thought for sure you were lost with it. He leaned back slightly against the table to alleviate his aching back. "What can this old man do for you?"

"You can come in now." she called behind her. A tall dark-skinned human with black hair braided in elegant dreadlocks stepped through the door. The black shirt he wore looked too small and it stretched taut over bulging pectorals and biceps. A green hue emanated in rhythmic pulses from where his heart should be. Baggy pants opened near his ankles with multiple tears in the cuffs. The shoeless feet were an oddity, especially for a Human.

As KarDel examined the being, his mind raced back to his time on Praug, and he instantly realized who stood before him. What stood before him. This wasn't a normal Human male. No, it was a scientific abomination of magic and man, created for one purpose: destroy the Aetherials.

Sensing the apprehension in his reaction, Tu'Mar pleaded her case. "We need your help. I need your help. Please."

That word. *Please.* Tu'Mar was never one to ask for help. If she needed help, there was a legitimate reason behind the request. He inhaled deeply and let out an exaggerated sigh, knowing he had no choice. "Alright, I'll help. But you owe me."

Technically, I owe you for saving my life, so maybe we can even this up once and for all.

The Tinkerer led the pair to an empty examination table on the other side of the room and they began their work.

# | 7 |

# The Will To Survive

*Approximately one year after the events of Chaos and Consequences*

Tobias watched as the man on the Holovid in front of him rambled quietly. It had been months since the Kai Stormbringer was captured; it had been almost as long that each day he was subjected to numerous forms of interrogation and torture. None were intended to physically kill him, but they were nonetheless excruciatingly horrible.

Yet still, somehow, he remained unbroken. Sure, he rambled aimlessly to the four walls around him. That was normal behavior for some of the inmates at Darklight Prison. This one was special, though. He was an Aetherial, one of the last of his kind, a lucky survivor to this point, a traitor to Emperor Tenon and the Aetherial Order. He had been banished after returning from a failed mission, where he left his fellow Aetherial brethren to die.

He was also Tobias' brother. Older brother, to be exact. Though he didn't much resemble it now. The muscles that once filled his brother's clothes had all but disappeared, leaving a shell of the man he once knew and trusted.

Now, Tobias resented his very existence. The brother who left him to die eighteen years ago, whose betrayal led to Tobias being trained under the watchful eyes of Emperor Tenon. His brother would never know the pain he suffered, the nights that felt like an endless nightmare; the despair and desperation as he struggled with unimaginable loneliness.

*It's your turn now, brother. It's time I made you feel the same way I have all these years. You left me, I trusted you, I loved you as my older brother, and you abandoned me. I hate you. I hate you with all the fibers of my being and every essence of Aether I channel.*

*You will never know how I felt. The horrors I've witnessed would drive any sane person to commit terrible acts. Hell, maybe I have already. Though, maybe you have as well. Maybe we aren't that different after all this time.*

A guttural scream from the video feed broke Tobias away from his thoughts. Perhaps that was for the best; they tended to get the better of him the deeper he sank into the depths of his subconscious mind.

The man on the projection ranted wildly, cursing, and vowing vehemently to kill this Endbringer, whomever he was. The verbal tirade continued, with the boney man standing and rising to his feet as he pointed a finger directly at the camera in the corner of his cell. Tobias didn't need to be in front of that room to feel his brother's anger. He felt it splashing through the Aether, like a boulder impacting with the ocean beneath it after it was launched from a mountaintop.

It filled Tobias with a strange satisfaction; one he rarely felt these days. His methods were working. Before long, his brother would break. He was so close now, as the screaming and barrage insults continued to fly, a slight smile curved his lips upward.

*All this time I thought I was the crazy one. Look at you. You're a raving lunatic in there. It's truly pathetic. I thought you were this mighty Captain Demico slayer. It's been almost a year and still that's all anyone can talk about. They may not see it, but clearly, that was just dumb luck, like most of your other victories in life. You may have a will to survive all this time, but you aren't the only one.*

A feeling manifested in the deep recess of his brain. It was foreign, uncomfortable, and unwelcome. After a certain point in his life, he forgot this was something one could feel. His eyes drifted away from the monitor and he sank away from the world around him; the feeling overtaking his entire being.

Guilt.

His smile immediately disappeared and his brows slanted in frustration. *I don't understand. If this is what I've wanted for so long, then why do I feel this fragment of guilt? It shouldn't be here. You left me to die, you bastard. I should not feel this way!*

*No, no, no! I will not allow myself to feel this way about you. You are a monster, Kai Stormbringer. Even if you don't see it, I do. No way in the six hells should I feel guilty about our situation. You had this coming. You deserve this pain the same way I deserved to have my own brother stay with me instead of fleeing like a coward.*

*A voice as quiet as the wind hissed softly in his mind. "You're better than him, you know. You overcame your challenges. This poor human will not ever become as strong as you. This is your true calling, Endbringer. You agreed to my bidding, do not forget that. We made a pact beyond mortal flesh and words."*

Tobias shook his head and the guilt out of it. He needed to snap out of it before his master snapped. *"Yeah, I remember. We have a deal. I will fulfill our pact, master."*

He turned over his wrist and pressed a few buttons on the revealed device under the cuff of his trench coat. A pleasant chirp sounded as it connected with one of the guards stationed outside the cell.

"Yes, Endbringer. Are you ready for the inmate?" a gruff voice answered from the other end.

"I am. Don't rough him up too much on the way over today.

"As you wish. We will have him strapped in momentarily." The call ended with a soft click of the transmission cutting off.

*Still not used to that trick. I don't know how he does it, and I don't think I want to anymore. Okay, let's get this over with then.*

He breathed in heavily and let his thoughts escape with a lengthy exhale. He stood up from his chair, turned off the Holovid, and tidied up his coat. As he tapped into the Aether, he felt the overwhelming ocean of despair and desperation from the millions of prisoners held within the Darklight Prison. If one were to unlock unnatural corruption and control of the Aether that was the Nekrofiends way, Tobias could think of no better place in the galaxy in which to do it. In Darklight Prison, sunlight was seldom, intense paranoia ran rampant among the inmates, and violence was just another act without a second thought among the common areas. The despair and agony permeated through the halls, cells, and security checkpoints scattered about the low orbit facility.

Those sensations were exactly what Tobias needed to center his mind. He refused to let weaknesses like compassion and sympathy or blood relations to erode the mental fortitude he had built up to this point in his life.

*I've overcome numerous tests of my will to survive. Come, brother, let us see who has the stronger will to survive while you're on the edge of madness.*

By day, he's a cybersecurity analyst. By night, he's the author of the Aetherial War series. As an avid lover of science fiction and fantasy stories, Nathan grew up mesmerized by Star Wars, and hoped that one day he could also create a universe as entertaining and fascinating. Now, he's proud to say that he has been able to live his dreams among the stars, and hopes others will share his passion and excitement for all the stories to come in the Aetherial War universe.

www.ingramcontent.com/pod-product-compliance
Lightning Source LLC
Chambersburg PA
CBHW071216300726
48975CB00004B/1328